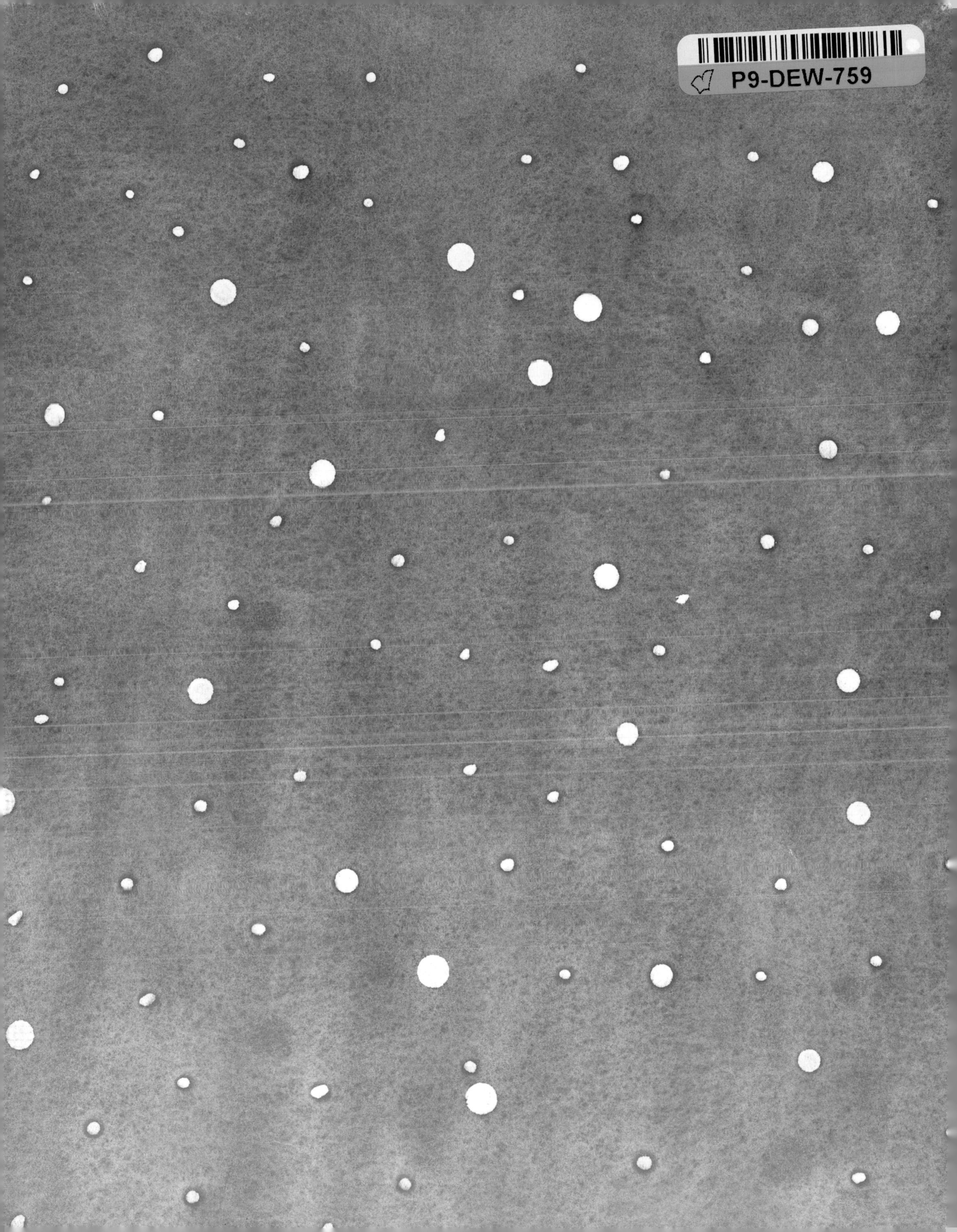

TO KRISTA, WHO KEEPS US ALL IN MITTENS

Thank you, Alexandra and Chloë, for the creativity and energy you put into nurturing this book into being.

SIMON & SCHUSTER BOOKS FOR YOUNG READERS
An imprint of Simon & Schuster Children's Publishing Division
1230 Avenue of the Americas, New York, New York 10020

Book design by Chloë Foglia
The text for this book is set in Century Schoolbook.
The illustrations for this book are rendered in watercolor on Arches 140-lb. hot-press paper.
Manufactured in China
10 9 8 7 6 5 4 3 2 1
Library of Congress Cataloging-in-Publication Data
Harper, Lee, 1960–
Snow! Snow! Snow! / Lee Harper.
p. cm.
"A Paula Wiseman Book."
Summary: A father and his two sons spend a perfect day sledding
together.
ISBN: 978-1-4169-8454-2 (hardcover)
[1. Snow—Fiction. 2. Sledding—Fiction. 3. Fathers and sons—Fiction.
4. Dogs—Fiction.] I. Title.
PZ7.H23139Sn 2009
[E]—dc22
2008051985

SNOW! SNOW! SNOW!

LEE HARPER

A Paula Wiseman Book
Simon & Schuster Books for Young Readers
New York London Toronto Sydney

One night
the wind howled,
and the snow fell
all night long.

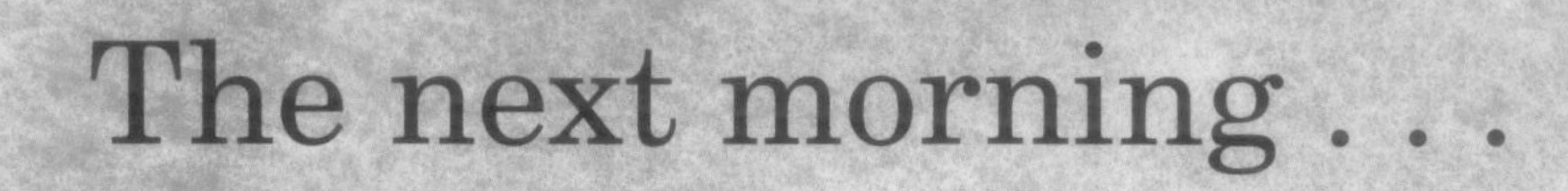

The next morning . . .

surprise!

It was the perfect sledding day.

We got ready
as fast as we could

and hiked to the lake

. . . where there is the
best sledding hill in the
whole
wide
world.

We made a triple-decker sandwich . . .

and swooshed down the hill
faster than the speed of sound.

Then we hit a BIG bump . . .

and shot into the air!

Up in the clouds . . .

we were flying.

"Uh-oh."

SPLO

OMPH!

"Again! Again!"

And back up the hill we went.